For Rebecca Flynn
W.M.

For Dr. Scott
P.B.

Copyright © 1984 by William Mayne
Illustrations copyright © 1984 by Patrick Benson
First published in the United States of America
in 1984 by Philomel Books,
a member of The Putnam Publishing Group,
51 Madison Avenue, New York, NY 10010.
First published 1984 by
Walker Books Ltd, London.
Printed and bound in Italy. All rights reserved.

Library of Congress Cataloging in Publication Data
Mayne, William
The blue book of Hob stories.
Summary: In five episodes, Hob, the friendly
household spirit, continues to make life
better for his human family.
[1. Fairies—Fiction] I. Benson, Patrick, ill.   II. Title.
PZ7.M4736Bn   1984   [Fic]   84-4231
ISBN 0-399-21037-7

THE BLUE BOOK OF
HOB
STORIES

WILLIAM MAYNE

ILLUSTRATED BY PATRICK BENSON

PHILOMEL BOOKS
New York

HOB AND CLOCKSTOP

"How strange," says Mrs., the last day of February, at time for tea.

"How strange," say Boy and Girl. "Hob has laid the breakfast table."

"Breakfast," says Mr. "What nonsense. If there was such a person as Hob he would have to go."

"Hob's mad," says Budgie.

"Hob is doing his best," says Hob. "They're late. It's breakfast o'clock by the Grandfather."

"Tock," says Grandfather. "Tick."

"The clock is wrong," says Mr. He tries to set it right.

The weights run down. The pendulum goes clatter. Something mechanical is the matter.

"Never mind," says Budgie. "I will ring my bell," and she rings half and quarter past twenty-seven o'clock.

At night Hob comes out.

"What's the trouble, Grandfather?" he asks. "Hob wants to know. Are you on strike?"

Grandfather groans. "I've chilblains on my hands," he says, "and a pain in my bell. I think I'm two days slow."

"You've run down," says Hob. He looks inside.

"Tick," says Grandfather. Hob puts a finger in.

"Tock," says Grandfather. "I think you've hit the place."

"Something has crawled in," says Hob. "It is tangled around your hickory dickory dock. It is a Clockstop."

"Oh, ding, dong," says Grandfather.

"Come out, Clockstop," says Hob. He pulls.

"I'm stopping here," says Clockstop, "eating seconds and minutes."

"I can spare a few," says Grandfather.

"I'll eat the hours and the days," says Clockstop.

"Take them and let me go," says Grandfather.

"I'll eat the phases of the moon," says Clockstop.

The pendulum falls off. "I'll eat the date," says Clockstop. "Whole years at once."

Then Hob remembers what date it is, what day.

"Don't be greedy, Clockstop," he says. "We all have to share. There's lots of us and we want a few minutes each."

"All right," says Clockstop. "I might get time-ache."

"Have today every time it comes," says Hob.

"Yum yum yes," says Clockstop. "Every year I'll come back." And out he comes, a long and springy, ringy thing. He goes away quite pleased with a handful of milliseconds to eat on the way.

"Tick tock, tick tock," says Grandfather clock. "I'm mended and I'm well, ding, dong, bell."

Hob gets a candle for a gift. "I could see to mend midnight now," he says.

Clockstop comes again next February 29th, in a leap year four years later. Hob worked it well. Clockstop is a long time gone.

HOB AND WUMP

In the night Hob comes from his cutch, his cupboard underneath the stairs.

"He does his good deeds then," says Boy.

"And gets a reward," says Girl.

Mr. says, "Nonsense."

But Hob comes out. Tonight he rocks the cradle. Baby has been cross all day and does not want to sleep.

Budgie rocks her cage and rattles.

Baby was going off to sleep. He wakes up again and whimpers.

"Hush, Budgie," says Hob. "Hush, Baby."

Budgie stamps about her perch.

"Shush," says Hob. "Hob is busy."

"It's not me," says Budgie.

Hob rocks the cradle. Baby forgets how cross he is. His eyes close.

Rock, rock, gently rock, goes the cradle. Hob feels sleepy too.

The cradle rocks faster.

Tap, tap, quickly tap, it goes.

"Not so hasty," says Hob.

Baby blows a bubble. Pop goes the bubble. Out comes a shout.

Bang, bang, trample bang, goes the cradle.

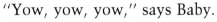

"Yow, yow, yow," says Baby.

Hob is out of breath. "Puff, puff, puff," he says. "There's more than Baby in the cradle."

Thump, thump, rockety thump, goes the cradle. Baby falls out. Hob catches him.

"I'll hold him," says Budgie.

"The bird is mad," says Hob. "But we have a problem here for Hob to solve."

Wump goes the cradle.

Cradle stops, but Wump goes on. Wump in the kitchen, Wump in the hall; Wump in the passage, Wump up the wall; Wump in the chairs, Wump on the stairs. Says Hob, "It won't do at all."

He puts Baby back to sleep. "Sing to him, hen," he says to Budgie.

"Go to sleep, little egg," sings Budgie.

"The bird's an idiot," says Hob.

Wump is wumping in the cellar.

"Why?" asks Hob. "This is my house."

"Looking for Grandwump," says Wump. "Mr. Earthquake. And there's Auntie Sonic Boom, and Cousin Noisy Neighbor, and my little sister Footsteps In The Night."

"They don't live here," says Hob. "Try down the road."

Wump climbs the cellar steps. The whole house shakes. Budgie's knees molt. Hob's teeth rattle. He opens the front door.

Wump goes out. Wump, wump, bumpety bump, down the garden path. His family calls to him.

Hob finds his present from Boy and Girl, an electric torch. While Baby sleeps and Budgie squawks, Hob puts back the seeds Wump shook out of the garden.

"Hob's work is never done," he says.

HOB AND HOTFOOT

"Hob will be cross," says Girl.

"But that is nonsense," says Mr. He is using a blue bowl to put dead matches in.

"We put our present for Hob in that," says Boy. "Hob is our household friend."

"Imaginary beings do not mind," says Mr.

Hob in his cutch, his den underneath the stairs, minds very much. Presents are presents, given, not bought. But if it's clothes, Hob goes.

That night he does not know what is his.

"All gone," says Budgie.

"You get your wages in birdseed," says Hob. "They're fattening you up. They don't keep you because they like you. They like me."

But the blue bowl is full of spent matches and nasty black stuff from Mr.'s pipe.

Hob picks up the bowl and puts it down. Hob is sad. Hob will do no work. Hob goes back to bed.

"Come out, come out," sings Budgie. "There's something about."

Hob will not come out. But the next day he is sorry when he hears the family talking.

"What dreadful marks," says Mrs. "How did they come?"

Hob wonders what she means. "Has Hob done it?" he wonders.

Something has been on table top and sideboard, cupboard top and floorboard.

White circles are lying everywhere. Hob finds them when he comes out. White rings appear on polished places.

"Hotfoot has been here," says Hob. "You did not tell me, Budgie."

"He has not been up here," says Budgie. But she is wrong. Hotfoot trod in her water and it boiled away.

Hotfoot walks across the washing hung to dry and burns brown rings in it.

Hob knows what to do. He goes for his blue bowl. Tonight there is a splendid gift in it, making up for yesterday. It is a sweet plum pie with a sugary crust.

Hob puts it on the table. It is still hot. It leaves a hard white ring. "Oh dear," says Hob, and eats the pie.

When it has gone he takes the bowl outside. It is the time for cold moonlight. He fills the bowl with that and brings it in.

"Warm up my custard," he says to Hotfoot.

Hotfoot comes to scorch the custard. He gets into the bowl, into the moonlight lying cold in the bowl.

Hotfoot freezes. Hotfoot turns solid with cold. Hob picks him out, and at the garden gate he rolls him down the road.

"That's a different sort of bowl," says Hob.

When Hotfoot has finished rolling he falls flat. In the morning workmen think he is a hole and put a lid on him.

In the house Hob washes all the marks away with moonlight. They go from desk and doorway, bench and stairway. All except the one Hob made himself, which will not scrub away.

"Hob's autograph," Hob says. "If I could write."

HOB AND DUSTY

Mrs. takes the carpet off the stairs and rolls it out on the garden path.

"I can't get the dust out of it," she says. Dust flies over the garden.

"Stop it," says Mr. "My cabbages."

"Hob might be in it," says Girl.

"Nonsense," says Mr.

Mrs. goes thump, thump, with a carpet paddle.

But Hob is in his cutch under the top step.

Boy and Girl go to look. They mean no harm.

The top step is loose. They do not mean to be impolite.

Hob hears the boards begin to rattle.

Boy and Girl do not mean to be unkind. They love Hob around the house.

Hob hears a nail begin to creak, creak, creak.

"Go back in your cage, Budgie," he calls. Budgie is offended. Hob thinks her voice is like a nail pulling out. She mutters like a clockwork bird.

Hob sees daylight coming in. He leaves the cutch through his own front door. He hides inside the Grandfather clock.

"Don't tickle, tickle," says the clock.

"This happens every hundred years or so," says Hob.

"I remember," says the clock. "It was a Tuesday." Budgie thinks it was last week. There was Tuesday then.

Boy and Girl have lifted up the step. Hob's little bed is hard and humpy, short and lumpy.

Beside it is a dusty floor. Dusty gets up and looks at Boy and Girl.

"We'll sweep it out," says Girl.

When they go for brush and pan Dusty climbs out and down the stairs. He is made of fluff, feather, threads and bits. He goes into a corner.

He leaves crumb, grime, dirt and grit wherever he goes.

Boy sweeps the cutch floor. Girl dusts Hob's things, his pipes and torch, his gifts.

They feel his wooden bed, his bony pillow.

They put the top step back. They clear the stairs of fluff and feather, they clear the floor of crumb and grime. Mrs. puts the stair carpet back.

Hob stays inside the clock all day. At night he comes out. He has some sweeping of his own to do. He has to be rid of Dusty.

Hob curls up in the dustpan. "Comfortable here," he says.

Dusty is molting hairy sand and grassy mud. Dusty climbs in beside Hob.

Hob carefully climbs out. Dusty shakes himself comfortable. Hob sneezes. Budgie sneezes. The clock sneezes midnight. Every sneeze means go. The door sneezes open.

Dusty sneezes. He falls to pieces. When he does, Hob picks up the dustpan and takes it outside before Dusty comes together again.

Dusty comes together too late, in the dustbin.

"This is home," says Dusty.

"Good night," says Hob. He goes in. Boy and Girl have left him a cushion for a pillow. He goes to bed.

HOB AND HICKUP

Boy and Girl have Puppy in the house. He runs about and barks at Hob's cutch or cupboard under the stairs.

"Come," says Girl. "Hob can't be nipped by you."

"I'd bite back," says Hob.

"Chase Baby," says Boy. "Baby thinks it's fun." Baby thinks it's fun.

"It's time for tea," says Mr. "Dogs outside. Give him a biscuit."

Girl gives him a pink one, Boy gives him a yellow one. Baby tries a pretty black one and drops it in a corner.

Then it is time for tea. Says Mrs., "Don't gobble it so quick."

Says Mr., "Hick." He's not the only one. Girl has Hickup too. Boy has such a big one they all laugh. Baby bounces up and down with it.

Boy gets a sugar lump with vinegar on it. He jumps on Girl and frightens Hickup from her.

Baby gets Hickup water made by Mrs. with a cinder from the fire.

Mr. has something from a bottle.

"That's best," he says.

"I could try that," says Hob.

"I don't believe in household spirits," says Mr., putting back the cork.

Boy and Girl and Baby, Mr. and Mrs. and Budgie, go to bed.

Hob comes out.

There is Hickup in the curtains. "Beg your pardon," says Spider, covering her face with all her legs.

"Hickory, dickory, dock," goes the clock.

Budgie says, "Skwee, skwee, skwee, skwee." She thinks she is singing. "Skwee, hick," she goes, and knows she's not.

"Hold your breath a couple of days," says Hob.

Budgie drinks from the back of her water pot and cricks her neck.

"Hick," go the taters in the cellar.

"Hack," goes the poker by the fire.

"Hock," goes the jam inside the jar.

"Huck and ill-luck," says Hob. "Who's there? Tell Doctor Hob."

Hickup comes up, and Hickup comes down. Hickup comes across the floor, hop, hick and jump.

"Stand still," says Hob.

"I can't," says Hickup. "I ate a pretty black biscuit behind the cradle, and we've all got it now."

"Stand still," says Hob. "STAND STILL!"

Hickup stands still. His little tummy goes hick and hock but he stands still.

"You've eaten dog biscuit," says Hob. "What's best for dogs?"

"Mmimm," goes Hickup, very quiet Hickup.

"Walkies," says Hob. And Walkies is what it is, by Hob's left heel and down the garden path.

"Now run away," says Hob, and Hickup does, hickover the road, hickover the hedge. People think Indigestion's going by.

Inside, blue Budgie blushes pink. She turns burple. "It wasn't Hick at all," she says. "I've laid an egg."

"Hob loves an egg," says Hob. "Hob does."

"If we weren't friends," says Budgie, "I'd sometimes hate you."

Hob eats his gift, a sardine on the bone.